THE KINGFISHER BOOK OF
MAGICAL
TALES

THE KINGFISHER BOOK OF
MAGICAL
TALES

Selected by
Sally Grindley

Illustrated by
Susan Field

KINGFISHER

NEW YORK

KINGFISHER
Larousse Kingfisher Chambers Inc.
80 Maiden Lane
New York, New York 10038
www.kingfisherpub.com

First published in hardcover in 1997
as *Breaking the Spell: Tales of Enchantment*
First published in paperback in 2002
2 4 6 8 10 9 7 5 3 1

1TR/1201/WKT/DIG(FR)/128MA

LIBRARY OF CONGRESS CATALOGING-IN-PUBLICATION DATA
The Kingfisher Book of Magical Tales / [compiled by] Sally Grindley:
[illustrated by] Susan Field.—1st American ed.
p. cm.
Contents: Dancing in the air / Joan Aiken—The paper garden / Tony Ramsay—The
Prince with three fates / Ann Turnbull—The snake princess / Jamila Gavin—
Chantelle, the princess who could not sing / Joyce Dunbar—The queen of bees /
Vivian French—The witch's ride / Jane Yolen.
1. Fairy tales. 2. Children's stories. [1. Fairy tales. 2. Short stories.]
I. Grindley, Sally. II. Field, Susan, ill.
PZ8. B673545 1996
[Fic]—dc20 96-3161 CIP AC

ISBN 0-7534-5388-6

Printed in Hong Kong

Contents

The Paper Garden

TONY RAMSAY

Along time ago, on a beautiful island that lay on the sea like a new moon, there was an emperor. He lived in a palace which looked out onto the loveliest garden in the East. It was a garden full of peacocks and cherry trees. It had a lake as smooth as glass. And most precious of all, lining its twisting paths, were rows of golden kushiri flowers, so rare they grew nowhere else in the world.

One day as the Emperor was sitting in his garden a breeze blew in over the kushiri beds and made their leaves rustle like paper kites. The Emperor sniffed the air. Then, bending low, he looked carefully at the lake which lay in the middle of his garden. What he saw made his nose wrinkle in anger.

"The wind!" he cried. "The wind is ruffling my lake!"

And sure enough the lake had changed. A moment before it had looked like a silver mirror. Now it was like a rumpled blanket where someone had been sleeping.

"Stop!" cried the Emperor, waving his fist at the wind. "Stop, I command you!"

But the wind cared nothing for emperors and continued to blow across the beautiful lake.

At once the Emperor summoned the imperial masons. "You are to build a wall," he said. "A wall so high the wind cannot enter my garden. If any man leaves a hole where the least draft can creep in he'll be buried alive!"

So the masons set to work and built a wall a hundred feet high from stone blocks carved so carefully even the blade of a knife could not slip between them.

And once again the most beautiful lake in the East looked up at the sky like a mirror.

For a time the Emperor was content. Then one morning while he was looking for peacocks (even then they were becoming difficult to find) a cloud covered the sun and rain began to fall. As it fell it pitter-pattered on the surface of the lake. And every drop made a circle that rippled outward until it reached the edge.

Once more the Emperor wrinkled his nose and grew angry.

"Stop!" cried the Emperor, waving his fist at the rain. "Stop, I command you!"

But the rain cared nothing for emperors and continued to fall on the beautiful lake.

This time he called his carpenters. "You must build a roof to keep out the rain," he cried. "And if any man leaves a hole where

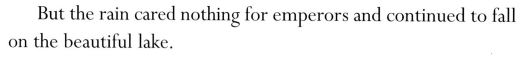

the least drop can creep in he'll be flung from the highest tower in the land!" So the carpenters set to work and built a roof of limewood over the garden.

But when the roof was finished no sunlight reached the lake and the flowers. The whole garden was dark as midnight. The carpenters were afraid the Emperor would be angry, so they chose the bravest among them to climb to the top and paint a yellow sun on the roofbeams. The paint was made of pure gold and shone down brightly on the lake below.

The Emperor was delighted. Now when he walked among the kushiri beds no breezes blew and ruffled the waters of the lake, and no rain pitter-pattered on the surface. He saw no peacocks now, but the lake was so beautiful he scarcely thought of them. But all was not well in the Emperor's garden.

Slowly the cherry trees began to lose their leaves. Leaf after leaf turned brown and fluttered to the ground.

Worse still, the kushiri flowers, which grew nowhere else in the world, had begun to shrivel. One by one they hung their heads and died.

The worried gardeners held a meeting in the summerhouse. All night long they argued until at last the chief gardener rose to his feet and said, "This is what we must do. We must cut flowers out of paper and paint them with the finest paints and stand them

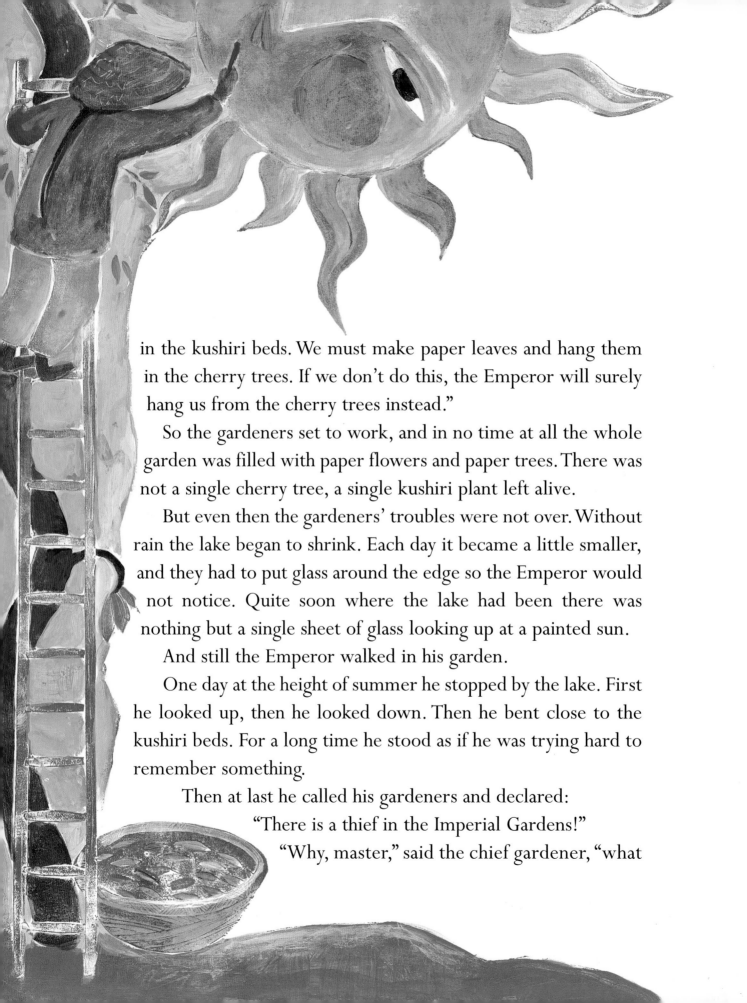

in the kushiri beds. We must make paper leaves and hang them in the cherry trees. If we don't do this, the Emperor will surely hang us from the cherry trees instead."

So the gardeners set to work, and in no time at all the whole garden was filled with paper flowers and paper trees. There was not a single cherry tree, a single kushiri plant left alive.

But even then the gardeners' troubles were not over. Without rain the lake began to shrink. Each day it became a little smaller, and they had to put glass around the edge so the Emperor would not notice. Quite soon where the lake had been there was nothing but a single sheet of glass looking up at a painted sun.

And still the Emperor walked in his garden.

One day at the height of summer he stopped by the lake. First he looked up, then he looked down. Then he bent close to the kushiri beds. For a long time he stood as if he was trying hard to remember something.

Then at last he called his gardeners and declared:

"There is a thief in the Imperial Gardens!"

"Why, master," said the chief gardener, "what

has he stolen?"

The Emperor glared hard
and his nose began to wrinkle.

"Someone has stolen the smell of
the most beautiful garden under the sun."

"No," said the gardeners, "it's not possible!"

"There is no smell," said the Emperor, "in the whole garden."

One by one the gardeners sniffed.

"It's very faint," said one.

"Almost not there at all," said another. "But I think . . . yes,
I'm almost sure I can smell something."

The Emperor wrinkled his nose and tried once more. Behind
him the gardeners were muttering to themselves. "Yes, yes, I can
definitely smell the cherry trees—or is it the kushiri flowers?
Yes, perhaps it is the kushiri flowers after all."

At this the Emperor went to the nearest of the kushiri
beds and sniffed hard. The leaves rustled as they always did,
like paper kites. But there was no smell. He went closer
and pushed his nose right into one of the flowers.

It was then something terrible happened.

The flowers had stood so long in the paper garden
they were covered in a fine dust.

And when the Emperor sniffed, the dust went up his wrinkled nose.

"A-a-a-a . . ." went the Emperor.

The gardeners froze with fright.

"A-a-a-a-a-a . . ."

Some of them turned to hide. But it was no good. A sneeze was coming.

"A-a-a-a-a-a . . ."

And no ordinary sneeze. A huge sneeze such as only emperors are capable of.

"A-A-A-CHOO!"

When the Emperor sneezed his terrible sneeze the garden suddenly changed. All the paper flowers and the paper leaves on the trees, every last one of them, fluttered to the ground. In a moment the most beautiful garden in the East had disappeared. In its place was nothing but a sheet of glass and some scraps of paper settling on the dust.

Now, when the Emperor saw what had happened to his garden and the gardeners told him how the peacocks had left and the kushiri flowers had died, he was deeply moved.

He ordered his workmen to take away the roof with the painted sun. He told them to pull down the blocks of stone so carefully carved you could not slip the blade of a knife between them. Then he told them to throw everything into the sea.

When that was done he returned to the spot where his garden had once been, the loveliest garden in the East, where the peacocks had lived and the last kushiri plant had died.

"I have been a fool," he said. "And now I will be remembered as the emperor who killed the last kushiri plant in all the world."

For a long time he stood by the glass lake and wept. Imperial tears slipped down his wrinkled nose and fell to the ground.

When night came, the Emperor returned to his palace filled with a great sadness. And there the sadness grew in him until quite soon he died.

But that is not the end of our story.

For where the Emperor had stood his tears seeped into the earth and there they touched a seed. And the seed swelled and put out a tiny shoot. And the shoot pushed upward through the dark earth until it peeped out at the sun. The shoot began to grow. And if you had been there and had listened very carefully, you would have heard a sound, a sound they thought had gone from the garden forever, a sound like the rustling of leaves. Or, like tiny paper kites flying in the wind . . .

Dancing
in the Air

JOAN AIKEN

A boy called Carlos lived with his mother in two rooms in the city of Barcelona, in Spain. His father, a sailor, had drowned at sea three years before. Carlos had no brothers or sisters. His mother went out every day to earn money by doing laundry for ladies in their houses. Carlos was left with a neighbor, Doña Rosa, who always told him to go out and play in the street.

So Carlos passed his days in the street, with his cat, Gat, who was thin as a rope and went everywhere wrapped round Carlos's neck.

In summer they watched the market women with their stalls of meat and fish and fruit and bread, or the ships along the harbor side. In summer the streets were warm, and Carlos and Gat were happy to wander. But in winter the city became very cold. Boy and cat hated the streets then, hated the rain and the snow and the wind that came hissing round corners. So, during those months they spent their days at the big church of Santa Eulalia.

They didn't go into the church itself, but into the cloisters next door. In the middle of these cloisters there is a square garden where quite tall trees grow; orange and lemon trees covered with fruit and flowers, and feathery palms, and at one side there is a big lumpy moss-covered fountain that trickles water all day and all night. The garden is enclosed by a low stone wall, and outside runs an arcade, a paved, roofed walkway where, in the old days, the priests and monks were able to take their exercise in bad weather.

This arcade made a fine place for Carlos and Gat to pass the days when the streets were windy and rainy and cold. Carlos settled himself in a corner, and practiced tunes on his fluviol. This was a little pipe, made of ebony, which had belonged to his father and his grandfather before him. He practiced hard, but quietly, so as not to disturb the priests going in and out of the big church.

And Gat? He squatted on top of the wall, like an ebony carving, and, with whiskers advanced and slitted eyes, watched over the geese.

There have always been geese in the cloister gardens of Santa Eulalia. They lead a very comfortable life growing fatter and fatter on food that visitors bring. Gat watched them all day, from his safe perch on the wall,

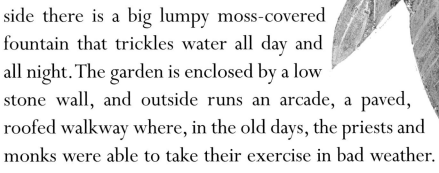

as they waddled about, and wove their long thick necks to and fro, and paddled with their yellow feet in the mud of the fountain.

Gat never interfered with them, nor they with him.

But one winter afternoon, the Bishop came into the cloister, very grand in red velvet and gold, with a big fur hat on his head. The Bishop was growing old, and his rich lunch had disagreed with him, and his feet hurt. He looked angrily at Carlos and Gat, and said to his secretary, "What are that boy and that cat doing in the cloister? Boy! Leave this place, you and your cat! The cloister is not a playground for you to play games in."

"Oh, please, but I wasn't playing games, only practicing my fluviol."

"Well, go and practice it somewhere else."

"Oh please, but it is so cold outside."

"Other people have to put up with that, and so must you," said the Bishop crossly.

As Carlos looked at the Bishop, suddenly a picture formed in his mind.

This was a thing that sometimes happened to Carlos.

Do you know how, once in a way, when you have a dream and wake up too quickly, you forget what you have been dreaming about, and the half-lost dream dangles inside you, like a tickle that you can't quite reach? The Bishop, that day, had woken too quickly from his after-lunch nap, and had left a half-finished dream somewhere behind him in the dark cupboards of sleep. If only he could grab the fringe of the dream and pull it out!

Carlos could see the dream quite clearly, floating at the back of the Bishop's mind. It was about a top, a beautiful red-and-blue painted top which the Bishop had lost when he was five. And in his dream he had been just on the point of remembering where it was. "I'll tell you! It fell into the well . . . " Carlos opened his mouth to say, but the Bishop said, "Quiet, boy!" and swung away, telling his secretary, "Make sure that boy leaves, with his cat, right away, and does not come back."

"Never?" pleaded Carlos, very forlorn, lifting black Gat off the wall. "Not ever?"

Faint strains of music, sounds of a band playing

cheerful tunes, reached them from the distance. But the noise of the band made the Bishop scowl even harder. It was playing music for the Sardana, and that was something the Bishop disliked even more than boys bringing cats into the cloister.

He spun round again, growing even angrier, as his aching, swollen feet gave him a sharp twinge.

"Not until people dance the Sardana one foot above the ground!" he snapped. "Not till then!"

And he limped peevishly into the church.

Carlos and Gat ran out the other way, through a door called The Door of Piety. Boy and cat made their way into the main square, the Plaza de San Jaime, St. James's Square.

There, because it was Sunday, people were dancing the Sardana to the music of a small band.

The Sardana is a special dance that people dance in Barcelona, and other towns in Catalonia. They have always done so, ever since the days of the old Romans, and very likely since long before that.

They throw their baskets and fans and jackets and bundles on the ground, then stand around their scattered things in a circle, holding hands. Their hands are high in the air. The circles of dancers can be large or small: three or four people, forty or fifty people, two hundred people. The dancers can be old or young, fat or thin, rich or poor. The people do not move around much, but stay in one spot, doing all kinds of clever, lively, bouncing steps, heel-and-toe, toe-to-knee, double-shuffle, feet-across-in-midair, heels-together, soles-together. Each step belongs to a special part of the music.

The whole square is full of dancing circles.

And the music? Very gay. Just to listen makes you want to join in a circle. People may go on dancing for hours and hours. Newcomers join in, others drop out when they are tired. The eleven-man band plays away for dear life on bagpipes and oboes and flutes and little drums. Then, at the finish, the dancing people will climb onto one another's shoulders, up and up, until they form a circular tower, a pyramid, with children at the peak. There they stand—just for a moment —till the music stops, and the whole tower comes dropping down again, like a pack of human cards.

Carlos loved the Sardana. He had been dancing it since he was able to walk.

Gat wasn't so keen. But he would sit by the band, on the steps of the town hall, with his paws tucked in and whiskers vibrating in time to the music.

After being turned out of the cloister, Carlos joined in the Sardana. He danced and danced. He thought: "I know why the Bishop doesn't like the Sardana. It's because his feet hurt. Even the thought of dancing makes them hurt. Poor old Bishop!"

As long as Carlos went on dancing, he felt sorry for the Bishop. But, after the dance had ended, Carlos began to feel very sad. It seemed so hard to be turned out of the cloister where he had been doing no harm.

Next morning, when Carlos and Gat had to trudge along the streets, it seemed even harder. The town was cold and busy and bustling, the wind blew keenly round corners, and Gat was in a bad temper. Gat didn't see why they could not go to the cloister.

Boy and cat wandered over toward the market. They passed a school, where the children could be heard singing.

"I wish I could go to school," thought Carlos. "The teachers there might show me how to play my fluviol better; and it would be warm in there too."

But he knew his mother could never find the money to send him to school. She made only just enough to pay for bread and milk and rent.

Just outside the market, which was held in a huge building with open sides, Carlos met a gypsy who had brought his goods into town on a donkey. The things he had for sale were all kinds of copper pans and jugs and kettles and cans. They had been polished hard, till they shone like brown jewels in the wintry sun; and they clanked as the donkey ambled along.

All of a sudden, Carlos had a flashing glimpse of the gypsy's dream.

The gypsy was a big, dirty, rather fierce-looking man with a whole bush of dark hair under a kind of turban, and a thick dark beard, and bright dark eyes, and gold rings in his ears.

"Oh, sir, I saw your dream!" cried out Carlos. "Had you forgotten about it? You were standing on the muddy banks of a big river—there had been a flood. Don't you remember? You were searching for your son. But he . . ." Now Carlos was sorry that he had started, but the strength of the dream had been too much for him, so he swallowed, and went on, "Your son had been drowned in the flood, he was washed over the dam. Do you remember it now?"

"Yes, boy. I do remember it now," said the gypsy, looking at Carlos very keenly. "I had forgotten it before, I couldn't reach it. So I thank you. You have done me a good turn. I think the dream was the voice of God telling me what became of my son, who was lost in a winter storm five years ago. I shall go to the church and

light candles and have prayers said for him. But how in the world is it, my boy, that you can remember somebody else's dream?"

"I can only remember when they forget them," said Carlos. "And not always then. And sometimes they don't want to hear them." He sighed, thinking of the Bishop.

"Well, you have unlocked the door for me," said the gypsy, "so I should like to give you something in return. Which one of these would you like?" And he waved a hand toward the glittering pans tied like a bunch of copper grapes all over the donkey's back.

"Oh, please, a kettle!" Carlos could hardly believe his luck. "Our old one was worn so thin that it leaked and put the fire out."

"There you are, then," said the gypsy, and he untied a kettle, not the biggest but a fair-sized one with a spout and a handle and

a lid. "There you are, and long may it last." The smile on his face was very friendly, so that Carlos, who at first had thought him rather a frightening man, now quite changed his mind.

"I'm going to give you these, too," said the gypsy.

From a pouch tied to his belt he pulled out a handful of brown strands, quite short ones.

"What are they?" Carlos was puzzled.

"Bits of hemp, that I use for tying my pots and pans to the

donkey's saddle. Put them in your pocket, you may find a use for them."

"Well, thank you, sir," said Carlos, still puzzled. "Bits of string always do come in useful, sooner or later."

"Yes, they do," said the gypsy. "Sooner or later." And he was laughing as he turned to lead his donkey into the market.

Carlos ran home joyfully, for his mother would be there by now, and he couldn't wait to show her the fine new kettle.

When it had been filled and set on the fire, Carlos discovered a surprising thing about it. As soon as the water in it grew warm, the kettle began to sing: a soft, dreamy, thready little tune, a queer clever little tune, that wavered up and down and made its own pattern.

"Do listen to the kettle, Mother!" he said.

But she, strangely enough, could not hear the tune. Only Carlos could hear it, and though he listened to it day after day, night after night, and tried to catch it on his pipe, he found it terribly hard to remember. He played and played, practiced and practiced, sitting on drafty piles of timber by the harbor, or on damp empty boxes outside the market.

Slowly, slowly, winter crept away and summer came back.

Every Sunday, people danced the Sardana. And Carlos danced too.

One Sunday in autumn, Carlos knew that at last he had really caught hold of all the ins-and-outs, the ups-and-downs, the forward-and-backward of the kettle's tune. He played it on his fluviol, once, twice, three times.

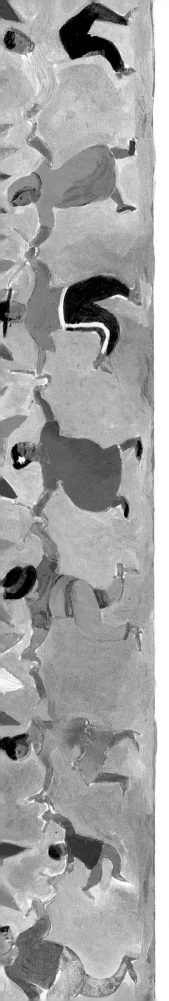

So, in the afternoon, when the band began tuning up in the square, Carlos left the two rooms where he and his mother lived.

"Carlos, come back!" she called. "I was going to mend your pocket!"

But Carlos, with Gat round his neck, had run into the street. As he crossed the square, the bottom of his pocket gave way, and all the strands of hemp that the gypsy had given him, and which he carried with him all the time, fell out and were strewn across the cobbles.

People, laughing, picked them up, and instead of holding hands, as usual, they held the ends of the short lengths of string, so that all the circles were linked up by the gypsy's little cords.

Carlos went to the leader of the band, Señor Miguel, and said to him, "Oh, please, sir, won't you play this tune for the dancing?"

And he played the kettle's tune very softly on his pipe.

"Play it again, a bit louder this time," said Señor Miguel, and he listened very hard, with his head cocked on one side.

"Now, play it again."

Carlos played it again.

"It is certainly a hard tune to catch," said Señor Miguel, but at last, after Carlos had played it about seven times, he and the other band players had caught it, and they all began to play it. Carlos would have left them then, and joined one of the dancing circles, but Señor Miguel said, "No, no, boy, you stay with us and play too."

So Carlos, bursting with pride, stayed with the band, on the steps of the town hall. And the people in the circles, holding the gypsy's bits of cord, began to dance.

Gat sat on the steps and watched.

The band played and played. The people danced and danced. And then a truly amazing thing happened. As the circles of people danced, bouncing higher and higher, they swung a little, first to the left, then to the right. And then—all of a sudden—every single one of the dancers, all the circles, large and small, all the people, fat or thin, were lifted right off their feet and up into the air.

Just for a few minutes, there they were, every single one of them, lifted off the ground, dancing in the air!

Just then the Bishop came round the corner, and he saw them.

Next moment they were all back on the ground again, laughing and cheering and throwing their hats in the air. And the gypsy's bits of cord had vanished clean away.

The band leader picked up Carlos and hugged him and said, "This boy has invented a tune that will last forever. You must play with us every Sunday, Carlos, and you must also go to school and learn music, and perhaps one day you will be the greatest musician in Spain."

But Carlos cried to the Bishop, "Sir, sir, they were dancing in the air! Did you see them? They really were! You must have seen them! So now may Gat and I go back into the cloister, please? May we?"

And the Bishop was obliged to say yes.

So that is why, if you go into the cloister of Santa Eulalia's big church in Barcelona, you are sure to see some geese by the fountain, and you will almost certainly see a thin little black cat watching them. That cat is Gat.

And Carlos? He became the greatest musician in Spain. But, sometimes, you may be lucky enough to see him in the cloisters too.

The Prince
with Three Fates
RETOLD BY ANN TURNBULL

Long ago in ancient Egypt there lived a king and queen who had no children.

The Queen prayed to the gods to give her a child, and at last a son was born to her.

Seven goddesses were there at the birth: the Seven Hathors, who would decide the child's fate. The goddesses gathered around the cradle, and said, "The prince will die young. A snake, a crocodile, or a dog will cause his death."

The King and Queen were brokenhearted. But the King believed he could save his son. He had a house built for the child in the desert, with servants to watch over him and make sure he never went outside.

The child grew. One day, when he was playing on the flat roof of the house, he looked down and saw a man walking along the road, and with him was an animal the boy had never seen before.

"What is that animal?" he asked.

The servant said, "It is a greyhound."

"Bring me one," said the boy.

"The King, your father, has forbidden it."

But the boy said, "I must have a greyhound. There is nothing in the world I want so much."

He sent messengers to his father, begging for a dog, and at last the King relented. "Let him have a puppy," he said. "Surely that can do him no harm."

So a puppy was brought to the Prince's house, and a jeweled collar was put around its neck, and it followed the Prince everywhere.

When the Prince was grown to be a man he said to his father, "I cannot live here hiding from fate. Let me go out into the world and take my chance."

Then the King was sad, but he gave his son a chariot with two horses, and the young man drove northward across the desert, taking with him only one servant and the faithful greyhound. And he decided to tell no one his true name until he had met his fate.

After many days he came to the kingdom of Mitanni.

Now the King of Mitanni had one child—a daughter—and he kept the girl locked in a room at the top of a tall tower and promised that any man who could climb the tower should marry her.

All the princes of Syria were camped around the base of the tower and every day they took turns to try to climb to the top. But the Princess of Mitanni did not want to marry any of the

princes of Syria, so every night, just before daybreak, she poured a jar of oil down the side of the tower below her window, and any man who came near was sent sliding down again.

One day the girl looked out and saw the Prince of Egypt at the foot of her tower. At once she fell in love with him. She said to her maid, "This one must not fail. Fetch me a rope!"

The Prince began to climb. The tower was slippery because of the oil, but the two girls let down the rope, and the Prince seized it, and climbed up, and sprang into the room.

The Princess hugged and kissed him, and said, "Tell me your name, and we shall be married."

"I am an Egyptian," said the Prince, "but I have sworn to tell no one my true name until I have met and defeated my three fates."

When the King heard that his daughter had been won by a foreigner who would not give his name, he was angry and said, "Send him away!" But the Princess said, "If my father does not let me marry this man, I will not eat, I will not drink; I shall die." The servants reported this to the King, and he grew angrier still, and sent men to kill the Prince. But the girl said, "If you kill him I shall be dead before sunset. I will not live an hour without him."

Then the King relented, and agreed to the marriage. And when he met the young man he loved him at once, and gave him a house and lands and treated him like a son.

The Prince told his wife about the three fates that threatened him. The girl was alarmed and wanted him to kill the dog. But the Prince said, "How can I kill this dog? He has been my companion since I was a child. He won't harm me." But still his wife was afraid.

One night when the Prince was sleeping, a snake came out of a hole in the wall and crept toward him. The Princess was watching. She brought a bowl of beer and offered it to the snake. The snake drank the beer. It drank so much it became drunk and rolled on its back. Then the girl killed it with an ax.

The Prince woke and saw the dead snake.

"I have saved you from the first of your fates," said his wife.

The next day the Prince and Princess were walking by the

that! It's going out on an adventure to find your fortune!"

"And breaking a spell and finding a prince," said the second princess. "But you're MUCH too stupid ever to do that."

"Yes," said the eldest, "MUCH too stupid!"

The Prime Minister coughed. "Excuse me, Your Majesties, but doesn't that rather prove my point?"

The King sighed heavily. "You're quite right," he said. "But is a quest the only way?"

The Prime Minister nodded. "Yes," he said. "Unless you want them here in the palace for ever and ever."

The King and the Queen looked horrified.

"A quest it shall be," said the King.

"At once!" said the Queen.

The three princesses were sent off on their quest the very next day. The two eldest moaned and complained bitterly, but the King and Queen were firm.

"You can come back as soon as you've finished," said the King.

"As soon as you've found your fortune and broken a spell and

found your prince," said the Queen. "I'm sure it won't take long." And she waved them good-bye from the top of the castle.

The two eldest princesses walked slowly down the road, huffing and puffing. The youngest danced in front of them, singing happily. Gradually the road grew more and more winding, and they found themselves in a strange land where the trees were bent and twisted and the grass was dry and dusty. The sun was going down, and the sisters began to yawn.

"Time to stop," said the eldest. She pushed the youngest. "Hurry up and find some sticks. We need a fire to keep us warm. I'm going to have a rest." She was about to sit down when the second sister screamed.

"Eek! Don't sit there! Look at all those HORRID little ants! "

"YUCK!" The eldest jumped up. "Let's squish them and squash them!"

"NO!" The youngest came running up. "Poor little ants!"

The eldest sister stared for a moment. Then she grinned. "All right. But only if you make us an ENORMOUS fire. AND find

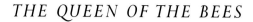

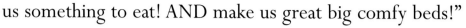

us something to eat! AND make us great big comfy beds!"

"That's right," said the second. "Because if you don't we'll squash and squish EVERY SINGLE ant!"

The youngest daughter scurried about. She built a fire, and she found sweet berries and nuts, and piled soft bracken and thistle-down into beds for her two sisters. When the two princesses were fast asleep and snoring loudly she sat down with a sigh.

"Thank you, Princess," said a teeny tiny voice.

The youngest princess looked all around. There was a tickle on her arm, and she saw an ant standing and bowing.

"Thank you for your kindness. If ever you have need of help, call for the King of the Ants, and I will help you!"

The two elder sisters were late up the next day. They said it was the youngest's fault for making their beds too soft, and they began arguing about where they should begin to look for fortunes and spells and princes.

"There certainly won't be anything round here," said the eldest. "There's nothing but boring old bushes and trees."

"No," agreed the second. "And boring old rushes and reeds."

"Rushes?" said the youngest. "Then there must be a stream!" And she ran to look.

"QUACK! QUACK!" A duck flew up into the air from under her feet. A flurry of ducklings scattered and hopped into the stream that was hidden under the bushes.

"QUICK!" shouted the eldest sister. "Catch them! We can have delicious duck for breakfast!"

"And duckling pie for supper!" said the second.

"NO! NO!" said the youngest sister. "Dear little ducklings!"

Her two sisters stopped and looked at each other.

"Hmm," said the eldest. "What will you do for us if we leave the ducks alone?"

"I'll make you breakfast! And supper! And soft, comfy beds!"

"Well . . . " said the second.

"I PROMISE!" said the youngest.

When the two eldest sisters had eaten their breakfast they lay down again. The youngest daughter sat beside the stream, watching the fluffy yellow ducklings bobbing on the ripples.

"QUACK!" said a duck, stepping out of the reeds. "Thank you, Princess. If ever you need my help, just call for the King of the Ducks!"

By the end of the day all three princesses were tired and hungry. They walked away from the stream and up and over a hill, and their feet were sore and their clothes were dusty.

"I can't walk a step farther," said the eldest princess.

"Nor me," said the second, and they flumped down on the ground under a tall tree. The youngest sat down too, but her sisters pulled her hair.

"We want our supper!" they demanded. "And we want it NOW!"

The youngest got slowly to her feet. There was a faint buzzing, and they all looked up. Hanging from a branch of the tree above them was a bees' nest.

"HONEY!" The eldest princess began shaking the branch. The bees buzzed angrily.

"HONEY!" said the second, and she shook the youngest sister. "Quick! Climb up and fetch us the honey! Beat the nest down! Do it NOW!"

"NO! NO! NO!" said the youngest. "Leave the bees! Please leave the bees!"

But her sisters would not listen to her. They hurried to fetch long sticks, and came crashing back through the wood waving them.

"NO!" said the youngest. "NO!" And she climbed up the tree and held the bees' nest in her arms. Bees flew all around her, but not one stung her.

The two eldest sisters looked at each other, and threw down their sticks.

"You'd better promise us something VERY special," said the second.

"VERY special indeed!" said the eldest.

"I'll find the fortunes!" promised the youngest princess. "I'll break the spells! I'll find the princes!"

"Very well, said the eldest sister. "But you'd better be quick about it!"

"That's right," said the second. "We're TIRED of questing!"

That night the youngest sister could not sleep. She climbed right up to the top of the tree, and looked out over the starlit land. The bees hummed about her, and a small voice buzzed in her ear.

"Thank you, Princess! Thank you! If ever you have need of us, call for the Queen of the Bees!"

The youngest sister smiled. "I'll remember." She climbed a little higher, and stopped. What was that she could see outlined against the night sky? She rubbed her eyes. It looked like a castle . . . .

The two eldest sisters were not pleased at being woken up.

"Quick!" called the youngest daughter. "I can see a castle! It must be the end of our quest!"

The three princesses reached the castle as the sun began to rise. The eldest knocked loudly on the door, and a little old woman opened it.

"We've come to find our fortunes and break the spells and rescue the princes, old hag!" said the eldest princess rudely.

"So let us in!" said the second.

The old woman nodded. She led them inside, and showed them a courtyard full of tall grass and weeds. All around were stone statues . . . statues of princesses. They looked surprised and angry—and very, very still.

"Excuse me," said the youngest princess, "but what are these?"

The old woman cackled. "Princesses, my dear," she said. "Come a-questing they did, but they couldn't break the spell.

The spell caught them instead!"

The two eldest princesses took a step back, and pushed the youngest forward. "SHE'S going to do the spell breaking," they said. "SHE'S the one who'll get turned into stone if she fails!"

The little old woman cackled again. "Too late, my dears! If she fails, you ALL get turned into stone!"

The two eldest turned round to run, but the door was firmly shut. They glared at the youngest. "You'd better get it right!"

The youngest sighed. "Where do I begin?"

The little old woman pointed to the grassy yard.

"Hidden in here are a thousand pearls," she said. "Find them all, and that's your fortune. Fail, and you'll be turned into stone!"

"And then?" asked the youngest.

The little old woman took her arm. "Look here," she said.

The youngest daughter looked down and saw a deep dark well, full of gleaming water.

"At the bottom is a golden key," said the old woman. "Find it, or you'll all be turned into stone."

"And then?" asked the youngest.

The old woman rubbed her hands together. "Then we'll see what we'll see! But you'll never find the key!" And she shuffled away.

The two eldest princesses sat down and burst into tears.

"We don't want to be turned into stone!" they wailed. "We want to go HOME!"

The youngest took no notice. She sat down among the poppies and daisies, and called, "King of the Ants! King of the Ants! I need you!"

Almost at once there was a faint rustling in among the long grasses as ants came hurrying and scurrying from all around. They came in twos and threes and fours, and carried with them the shimmering pearls.

The youngest daughter sat and counted, and in only an hour all the pearls were heaped at her feet.

"Thank you, thank you!" she called, as the ants scurried away.

The old woman was not pleased at the youngest princess's success. She grunted as she took her to the well, but the princess smiled as she knelt down beside the water.

"King of the Ducks! King of the Ducks! I need you!"

"QUAAAAAAAAAAAACK!" There was a flurry and flapping of wings, and the King of the Ducks landed with a loud splash. He winked at the youngest princess, and dived deep, deep down into the well. In no time she had the dripping golden key on her lap.

"Thank you, thank you, King of the Ducks!" she called as the duck beat his wings and flew away.

The old woman took the key. "You must come this way," she said, and unlocked a huge golden door. The youngest princess followed her, and the two eldest princesses came behind, snuffling.

Behind the golden door was a huge golden hall, and in the hall was a great stone bed. Lying in the bed were three princes, as like one another as three peas.

The two eldest princesses clapped their hands as they looked.

"So HANDSOME!" whispered the eldest.

The second sister pinched the youngest. "Wake them up!"

The old woman cackled again. "Not so fast! Stone they are, and stone you'll be if you choose wrong!" She turned to the

youngest princess. "One ate sugar, one ate syrup, and the youngest ate honey before they were enchanted! Now, choose the youngest!"

The youngest princess walked slowly over to the bed.

"Queen of the Bees!" she whispered. "Queen of the Bees!"

There was a gentle humming, and in through the open window zigzagged the Queen of the Bees. She flew over the three princes, and settled on the nearest. The youngest princess sat down on the bed and put out her hand.

"This is the youngest prince!" she said.

At once there was a rush of wind, and the sound of hurrying feet and chattering voices as the stone princesses leaped back into life. They burst into the golden hall, but as they did so the bed gave a hop and a skip and a jump and soared up and out of the window. The two eldest princesses were only just in time to snatch at the covers and hang on tightly.

The King and the Queen and the Prime Minister were walking in the royal garden when the bed landed with a thump! beside them. The two eldest princesses picked themselves up and dusted themselves down. The youngest was still sitting on the bed, holding the hand of the youngest prince. They were smiling happily at each other.

"Well, well!" said the Prime Minister. "Welcome back!"

"We've found our fortunes!" said the eldest princess, and she tipped the thousand pearls out of her pockets.

"AND our princes!" said the second, pointing to the bed.

The two elder princes sat up and bowed.

"So glad to meet you," they said, and lay down again.

"Aren't they HANDSOME!" said the eldest princess proudly.

"Indeed we are," said the eldest prince. "We are as handsome as the moon and the sun together!"

"Exactly so," said the second prince. "And now—bring us our breakfasts!"

The Witch's Ride

JANE YOLEN

Agnes Browne lived in Gilsborough in the County of Northampton, of poor parentage and poorer education. She was born to no good, her neighbors said, never in the way of receiving any grace, nor wanting it. She was spiteful, they said, and malicious. Ugly, too. So they called her a witch, though she wasn't one.

Emily Early also lived in Gilsborough, and a blithe-looking girl was she. Always smiling and laughing, as if every living thing told her an amusing tale. She had golden hair and a golden disposition, and if ever grace shone on a spirit, it was on hers, or so said her neighbors. But unbeknownst to them, Emily Early was a witch and she practiced her dark arts secretly and alone.

Now, one day in summer two black cats wandered through the streets of Gilsborough, yowling and howling as if looking for trouble. They fetched up by Agnes Browne's rude cottage and sat there for a while, preening one another and passing the time. Anon they set off again, once more yowling.

It was right after this that Mistress Goody's baby daughter, Charity, went missing. The milk curdled in Mistress Dwight's churn. Three black crows flew west over Squire Danforth's field

47

and immediately his prize bull escaped from its meadow.

A crowd gathered quickly at Agnes Browne's door, where so recently the two black cats had been seen gossiping. A mob reasons with rumor. They called Agnes forth, trampled her flowers, and pulled the latch from her door.

She came out, her spiteful tongue wagging. "Clear off my stoop and out of my yard, you ill-bred ninnywits!" It did not help her cause that she spat as she spoke.

They bound her tight with the binding of the three narrows: wrists, elbows, knees. Then they dragged her to Witch's Hill, a place of dreadful inquiry. And there, though Squire Danforth's bull was soon caught, though Mistress Goody's Charity was found in the henhouse cracking eggs, there they named poor Agnes Browne a witch. Three witch-hunters were brought in from London to question her, and at last she confessed. She said that the two cats were not cats at all but familiar spirits named Bobbin and Drew. And having confessed, she was given a quick death, too quick for her to repent, but not so quick that she could not call down a curse on them all.

"All this town," she cried as the flames took her, "will come to no good of this." She was spiteful to the end.

Watching from the crowd, Emily Early smiled.

The squire himself died soon after, from a fall off his horse. And though the townfolk talked about it, they did not talk long. The squire was known to like his drink and had often taken a spill.

So the squire's son, Ewan, took over the estate, with his mother to run things as she always had. Ewan was a handsome, big boy, not overly bright. He had inherited his father's brains, though he would have done better with his mother's.

One day in this same summer Ewan saw Emily Early walking through the fields of wheat, her hair yellow as flowers. In that very moment he fell in love, as if struck by lightning. And though she was not of the gentry, he determined to marry her.

His mother had misgivings about the match, but Ewan was not to be denied. By summer's end the two were wed, and the widow Danforth moved into the dower house on the estate, leaving the newlyweds the fine big house.

Now, Widow Danforth kept her own counsel. She loved her son but was not blind to his faults. Neither was she charmed by his new wife. So when Ewan came to her one morning in late fall, she was not surprised.

"Mother, I sleep the night through," he said, "but I wake more tired than when I lie down. I fear I may be dying."

Indeed he looked it. His handsome cheeks were now sunken, and he seemed twice the age his father had been when he died.

His mother gave Ewan tea and stroked his brow and told him to bide with her a bit. She tucked him into a bed and left him to sleep the morning away, but herself she took off to the village priest.

The priest shook his head. "Call the doctor, madam," he

advised. "It is no matter for me."

"And if it be witches?" asked Widow Danforth.

"The witch is dead in the cleansing fire," the priest said, and would hear no more from her, for he thought she was just a widow pushed out of her house by the new wife and come to complain.

Having got no good of the priest, Widow Danforth determined to watch the night at her son's bedfoot to see if Agnes Browne haunted him. Or if—as she really suspected—the damage was inflicted by his bride. So she sent her son back home, and waiting until he and Emily were at their dinner, sneaked up the back stairs and hid herself behind the bedchamber curtains.

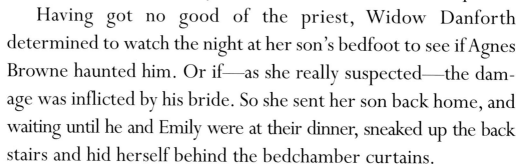

It was a long time till they came to bed. The night was dark and starless. Widow Danforth could scarcely see. But she waited patiently till all was quiet and both husband and wife slept as one.

Suddenly, a candle flared to light. And Emily Early, her yellow hair spread about like a halo, rose out of the bed. She passed her hand once, twice, then a third time over the flame. She whispered something that Widow Danforth could not quite hear, then turned to her sleeping husband. Leaning over him, she blew into his mouth.

Eyes still closed, Ewan rose and stood silent by the bedfoot.

"Higgety, hoggity, let me ride,
Saddle and bridle by my side,"

said Emily distinctly.

At once the sleeping man got down on his hands and knees as if he were a horse, and Emily straddled him. She whipped the

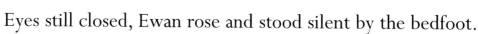

cord off her nightdress and put it through his mouth like a bridle, and he turned into a horse. Then she jammed her heels into his sides, and they were away, the girl on the blue-eyed steed out the door, down the stairs, and lost to sight.

"Well!" said Widow Danforth, stepping out from behind the curtains. "And here's a pretty pickle. Emily has enchanted my son and

ridden him off like a prize stallion—to a witches' meeting, I have no doubt of it. But what I can do to help my dear boy, I do not know."

At last daylight came, a pink thread of light stretching from hill to vale. And back they came, rider and ridden, clattering up the stairs, through the door, and to the bedfoot, where Emily took the cord from her husband's mouth and tied up her nightdress, whispering:

"Hoggity, higgety, let me sleep
Ten miles wide, a lifetime deep."

Then she slipped easily into the bed and drew the covers around

her, while poor Ewan, back in his own shape, lay down where he was on the floor, too tired to go even one step farther.

A second night the widow watched, and it was the same. But on the third, Emily Early was so full of herself that she spoke loudly over the flames like this:

> *"Fire to water, water to air,*
> *Make me a horse my weight to bear."*

And when the two had galloped away, Widow Danforth went to her own bed eagerly, saying, "Now I've got you, my girl."

That day Ewan visited his mother again, his blue eyes that used to be the color of dawn now the color of dusk. "I have come to make my peace with you, Mother," he said, "for I am not long for this world."

"Nonsense," said his mother, "you are but bewitched."

"Bewitched?" His puzzlement was all in the one word.

So she told him what she had seen, but he would have none of it. "My Emily is sun and moon," he said. "You have mistook her for old Agnes Browne."

"I will prove it," said his mother. "Take no food this night. No drink, either, for I believe she has set you a potion in them to make you sleep the sounder. But put you a potion in her meat and wine, and I will show you what she does."

So that very night Ewan pretended to eat and drink, but he put a sleep draft in his wife's food. And when it came time for bed, he laid himself down as if to sleep and was quickly snoring. His young wife lay down by his side.

No sooner was the girl asleep than Widow Danforth crept
from behind the curtain. She lit the candle and three times passed
her hand over the flame, saying:

> *"Fire to water, water to air,*
> *Make me a horse my weight to bear."*

Then she turned and leaned over the bedside and blew into Emily
Early's mouth.

All this Ewan watched from the bed, without a word.

Emily stood and went to the bedfoot, where she waited, eyes
closed, as patient as any mare, on her hands and knees.

"Get up, my son," Widow Danforth said, "and take the cord from
her nightdress. Then place it in her mouth as if it were a bridle."

Ewan did as she bade, but most reluctantly, for he feared to
hurt his pretty wife.

"Now get astride," said his mother, "and give her a kick."

"I cannot," Ewan said.

"You must," remanded his mother. "For you must ride off and
see where she goes. Only be sure to return by first light."

So he gave the yellow-haired mare a kick, just a tap, and they
were away, out the door, down the stairs, and out of sight.

When they returned at dawn, Widow Danforth
was waiting.

"Oh, Mother," Ewan said, "I was wrong to doubt
you. She is a witch as ever there was one."

He climbed off Emily's back.

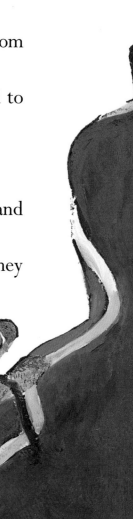

"We galloped up one side of Bald Mountain and down the other. And there was a meeting of witches, all sitting atop their steeds. And when they saw me they cried out, 'Where is Emily, who is always so early?' And I answered, 'She is off to another meeting and sent me in her place.' That seemed to satisfy them, for they did not ask again."

"Well done, my son," the widow said. "You have more than your father's brains after all."

Ewan took the bridle out of his wife's mouth. "But what shall we do about her?" he asked.

"Why, nothing," his mother said. "There is nothing we can do."

"But she is a witch and must be punished."

"There has been punishment enough in this town already," his mother answered. "And she will serve better as a mare than ever she did as a wife. Besides, in all the excitement I have forgotten the words to change her back."

It was the one lie Widow Danforth ever spoke, but she never repented of it, especially in the years that followed, when Ewan married again and she had seven grandchildren to teach to ride the yellow-haired mare in her son's fine stable.

The Snake Princess

JAMILA GAVIN

Along the banks of the Dal lake, all shimmering with lotus flowers and waters as smooth and limpid as the sky above, lived the snake princess. She loved to glide along its banks, weaving her sleek, elegant body in and out of the tall reeds, or lie coiled up in a sunny patch from where she could watch the boats sliding by and hear the voices of mankind.

Often, if the humans came too close, she would have to hide. Why did they hate her so much? She never set out to harm them. Only if one got in her way might she shoot out her venomous tongue—but it was just to protect herself. Mostly, she slept under boulders through the heat of the day and only came out in the cool of evening to hunt and quench her thirst in the lake.

One day while she lapped at the water's edge, a reflection broke over her across the waters, glistening with the rays of the setting sun. She halted her drinking and froze so still that her body blended invisibly with the reeds and the long grasses.

The reflection was that of a hunter. Wearily, he tossed down his bow and arrows and waded into the soft, silky waters of the

lake to drink and wash away the dust and grime of a day's hunting. The snake princess observed him as he cupped his hands and gulped, then dashed water over his face and arms. At first she was terrified he would see her and immediately kill her, so she hardly dared move, but when she saw how noble and handsome he was, she fell deeply in love with him.

Other hunters then came rushing down in their tramping boots and weapons of death, so she slid rapidly away and hid behind a rock. She heard them shout out to each other. "My, this is a wonderful spot. There cannot be a place on earth more like paradise than this—except, of course, Your Majesty's garden!"

Your Majesty? The snake princess elongated her body to see which one was the "majesty"—and then she realized it was that first hunter with the noble, handsome face.

"Yes," said the King, "this place is like paradise. Let us make our base here and stay a day or two."

At this moment, one of the hunters spied her. "Hey! Watch out! A snake!" and he hurled a spear at her. But the snake princess was too quick and escaped, like a ripple of water, into the reeds.

The next evening, when the hunters returned from their chase, once again the King came down to the water's edge to drink and bathe.

"Watch out for snakes!" warned his men.

The King was about to wade into the waters, when he heard a soft crying. It seemed to come from a grassy inlet almost hidden by the long thick reeds. Quietly, he stepped forward, parting the high stems with his two hands. There, sitting on a rock, was the most beautiful maiden he had ever seen. The way she sat—with her body coiled beneath her and her head bowed into her hands, and her long black hair hanging loose and shining like a summer's night—caught his heart.

"Madam, are you all right?" he called politely.

She lifted her face—her beautiful face with its full red mouth and almond-shaped eyes as green as the grass, and her honey-colored skin on which the lake rippled reflections, so that she looked as if she had been made of earth and grass and water.

She looked up at him with her brimming eyes and shook her head helplessly. There was no one else around, apart from his companions, so deciding that she was in distress and in need of help, the King flung a cloak around her and lifted her onto his horse. "Come back to my palace until you have recovered," he said.

The Princess looked at him with gratitude and nodded her acceptance. The King took her home, where she stayed, and stayed. Even when she was well again she stayed and when it was obvious that this strange beautiful woman was entirely alone in the world, the King lost no time in marrying her, and for a while thought he was the happiest man on earth.

But people began to notice: his friends and relatives, his courtiers and ministers, they all remarked that although his beautiful wife was the center of his universe and that all other matters took second place, somehow he didn't seem to be himself. His face took on a pale almost greeny tinge, his eyes often seemed hard and fixed and never blinking. He became cold and difficult to talk to.

One day, the King was out walking alone through his gardens, when he was astounded to come across a strange man fast asleep beneath a flowering fruit tree. He slept with a full pitcher of water nearby and an apple clutched in one hand. In the other hand, he held something the King couldn't quite see, because it was so small and enclosed tightly in the sleeper's fingers.

The King, who was at first about to be angry and have the trespasser ejected from his gardens, became curious. The exhausted man was so deeply asleep, he wasn't even aware of the King bending over him and loosening the object from his grasp. It was a small silver box, in which he found, when he opened the lid, a sticky sweet ointment. He sniffed it wonderingly.

At that moment, the stranger woke up.

Muddled with sleep, he leaped to his feet and went to pick up the water pitcher. He looked at the one hand which clutched the apple—and then at the other. When he saw his other hand was empty, he gave a howl of distress.

"Oh my goodness! Oh my gracious! I've lost my ointment. What will my master say? What will my master do?" He wailed and moaned as he hunted high and low.

The King felt sorry for him and stepped out saying, "Is this what you are looking for?"

"Oh yes, sir, yes, yes it is!" replied the stranger joyfully.

"I'll return it to you on condition that you tell me why this little box is so important," said the King.

So the stranger told him: "I am the servant of a venerable yogi —who is the holiest and wisest man in the world and who desires never to be without a jug of sacred water from the source of the River Ganga. This magic ointment enables me to travel to and fro at great speed without coming to any harm so that my master is never without this precious water."

"Hmm," murmured the King. "Is he really the wisest man in the world?"

"Oh yes," the servant assured him. "There is nothing in this world or the next that he does not know. There is no question he cannot answer."

The King thought about all the questions he wanted answers to, such as why was his skin turning scaly with strange zigzag patterns? Why did his blood seem to have turned cold? Why did he no longer like the light of day, but prefer, far better, the nights?

"Return to your master and tell him that if he wants his ointment, he must come and get it himself," commanded the King.

The servant, grateful at being allowed to leave without punishment for his trespass, set off immediately for home. But because he was without the magic ointment, it would take him a full two years before he arrived and was able to give his master the King's message.

The yogi was distraught at the prospect of being without a constant pitcher full of holy Ganga water, and so, with his servant set off to visit the King and get his ointment back.

Meanwhile, the King became more and more pale, and his eyes were now like two hard pebbles. His body was undergoing a terrible change, and deep in his soul he felt an unexplained terror. His skin had become so scaly and slithery that he hardly went out by day anymore so as not to be seen. Everyone shunned him as if he had a terrible disease. Only his mysterious wife seemed thrilled at the change in her husband. She often rubbed her limbs

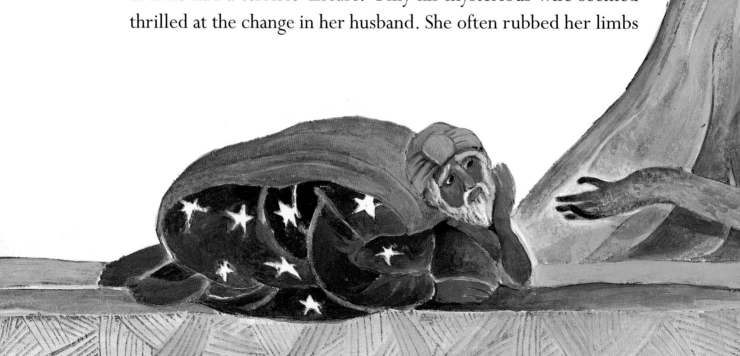

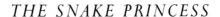

up against him and hissed softly in his ear, "Now we are becoming two of a kind."

When at last the yogi and his servant arrived at the palace, the King shielded himself behind silken curtains. "So, you have come at last to claim your ointment?"

"Yes, if it please Your Majesty," replied the yogi softly.

"Your servant says there is no question you cannot answer, so first tell me: why do I look like this?" The curtain quivered as a long green scaly arm protruded from it, coiling and twisting in the air. "Why do I prefer the night to the day? And why does my blood always feel cold? Answer me these questions and you shall have back your ointment box."

"Tell me, sire, when did your skin start to turn green? When did you start to feel cold and afraid?"

The King sighed sadly. "It is since I married a beautiful strange woman," he said, and he told the old yogi how he met his wife by the lake and brought her to his palace. "I love her more than all the world, but I don't know what is happening to me."

The yogi immediately cried out, "Oh sire! That is no

woman you have brought into your palace, she is the fearful snake princess. You must get rid of her immediately. Don't you see? You are turning into a snake!"

The King was outraged. "Do you dare to call my wife a snake? I'll have you whipped!" And he yelled for his guards to drag the yogi away.

"I can prove it, sire!" cried the yogi. "Believe me, if you do not do as I say, you will surely become a snake like your wife."

Although seething with upset and rage, the King agreed to let the yogi prove it to him. "If you fail, I shall have you put to death!" he declared.

"Prepare two kinds of kedgeree," instructed the yogi. "One sweet and the other salt. Place both kinds in one dish, but be sure that she only eats the salty portion. Finally make sure there is no drinking water anywhere in the palace."

That evening for supper, the King had the dish prepared, and when he and his wife sat down to eat from the one dish, he turned the salty portion toward her.

"Watch!" whispered the yogi. "The salt will make her thirsty and she will be forced to find water." The yogi knew that if the Queen went out at night, she would turn back into her snakelike form.

The King and his wife went to bed, but in the night, she awoke with a terrible thirst. She roamed the palace looking for a drink, but there was not one drop, so now she was forced to go out into the gardens and drink from the fountains. In horror, the King saw the dreadful sight; he saw his beloved wife turning into a long, slithery sliding snake with mottled, green, scaly skin. She coiled out across the grass, her tongue darting out as it searched for water.

"What shall I do?" he whispered hoarsely. "How can I save myself?"

"The powers of the snake princess are extraordinary, but there is a way," said the yogi and he began to explain.

The next day, the King, struggling to look as normal and loving as he could, suggested to his wife that they should do their own cooking today. They would light the oven and bake their own bread.

The oven, however, was to be a special oven. According to the yogi's instructions, it was made of many different kinds of metal and it was fixed to the ground by a powerful chain that even an elephant couldn't break.

Perhaps it was his last day of happiness—the King would never be sure; but for some hours, he and his beautiful wife roamed the gardens chasing and playing and laughing.

"Must I do this deed?" he whispered.

"Unless you want to become a snake, you must," answered the yogi.

So the King led her toward the oven which had been heating up in preparation for the baking and asked her to knead the dough. When the Queen had kneaded the dough and molded it into loaves, he opened the oven door and told her to put them inside.

The heat of the oven was so powerful that she could hardly approach it, but she obeyed her husband and, leaning forward, thrust the bread inside. At that moment, he leaped behind her and pushed her in as well and slammed shut the door, locking it and double locking it.

For hours, the snake princess used every power and spell she knew to free herself. The oven rocked and bounced and the great chain rattled and stretched with the strain. But it did not give way.

At last, the rocking stopped and all was quiet. The yogi made the King wait until the oven had cooled, then they opened it.

Inside was a great pile of gray ashes—all that was left of the snake princess. Except that among the ashes was a strange, round, whitish greenish stone. The King picked it up and with tears in his eyes, held it for a moment in the palm of his hand.

"That is the heart and soul of the snake," said the yogi. "Keep it. It has special powers and could make everything you touch turn to gold."

But even though the King felt the blood rush warm through his body, and the green mottled scales fell from his skin, his heart was full of grief. No amount of gold could bring back his happiness. He left the palace and rode down to the lake where he had first met the beautiful snake princess. He stood for a while staring out across the silky, limpid waters; he glanced at the reedy bank where he had first heard her cries, then with a breaking heart, he took the snake stone and hurled it as hard as he could, out across the lake.

It arched upward, spinning and twirling and sparkling, till finally, like a falling star, it plunged into the waters and sank for ever.

Then the yogi took back his magic ointment and, with his servant, departed from that sad place.

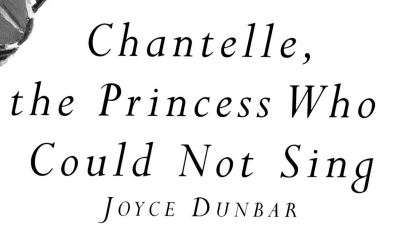

Chantelle, the Princess Who Could Not Sing

JOYCE DUNBAR

Once upon a time there was a princess called Chantelle. She was as beautiful as she was good, as good as she was graceful, as graceful as she was kind. But the most enchanting thing about her was her voice, and people loved to hear her sing.

When the princess reached the age of fifteen, a party was held in her honor. All the guests came with good wishes. All except one—a peevish aunt who was jealous of Chantelle. "Why should this slip of a princess have so much?" she grumbled to herself. And instead of giving her a good wish, this jealous aunt cast a spell so that when the princess started to sing, her beautiful voice was spirited away and let loose out of the window.

"There," cackled the aunt. "Sing away."

From that day on, the princess could not sing at all. Not a high note, nor a low note, not a la-la, nor a tra-la: whenever she tried to sing, the sound that came out of her beautiful throat was flat, flat as a doormat.

"I can't understand it," said the Queen.

"She used to have such a sweet voice," said the King.

As for Chantelle herself, it was clear from the way that she screeched and squawked so happily around the palace that she simply did not realize. She had become completely tone deaf. The King and Queen hired the best music teachers, but they all gave up in despair. And rather than offend by telling her to be quiet, the King and Queen and courtiers covered their ears.

Now it so happened that a handsome prince came to seek Chantelle's hand in marriage. He had heard all about the beautiful princess with the beautiful voice who so much loved to sing. But because no one talked about it, he hadn't heard that she could sing no longer.

As soon as the prince and princess met, they fell straightaway in love with each other and were betrothed. A celebration banquet was held and everyone ate, drank and was merry. It seemed there could never be a happier couple.

At the end of the banquet the prince turned to the King. "Your Majesty," he said, "I cannot tell you how happy I am to be marrying your lovely daughter, so renowned for her lovely voice. You know that my court is famous for its music, and as you can see, I have brought my lyre. What could be a more fitting end to this occasion than that the princess should accompany me in a song?"

An embarrassed silence fell upon the court. But the princess wasn't embarrassed, not a bit. Smiling, she rose to her feet. The prince began to play and the princess opened her mouth to sing . . . but oh, what a dreadful noise she made—it was flat, flat as a doormat.

The prince stopped his playing in astonishment. Then a pageboy began to titter, then a serving maid, until the whole court fell about laughing. But this was no joke. While the princess trembled and blushed crimson, the prince frowned. He could not possibly take such a princess as his bride—she would turn his court into a laughing stock! Muttering his excuses, the prince decided to return home. "I'll come back in a month," he said, "but make sure the princess has some singing lessons."

Poor Chantelle ran from the palace in tears. She found a hiding place among the bulrushes that grew by the royal lake and sobbed and sobbed, until at last a frog heard her and asked what the matter was.

"A handsome prince wants to marry me and he asked me to sing for him. But he didn't like my singing. Neither did anyone else. I can no longer sing a note," she sobbed.

"Don't you worry," said the frog. "I've a very fine voice myself. Meet me every morning at daybreak and I'll soon teach you to sing again."

And so, each dawn for a month, the princess had singing lessons from the frog. She made excellent progress, and when the prince made his promised return, the frog told her she was sure to please him.

Once more a banquet was held, and this time the prince brought his lute. He plucked a few notes and the princess began to sing. But the sound that came out of her beautiful mouth was . . . well . . . a passionate, full-throated C-R-O-A-K!

Of course the whole court fell about laughing; all except the Frog King, who followed the sound from the royal pond and fell straightaway in love with the princess.

Again, the prince made his excuses, promising to return in a

month, while Chantelle ran away in tears. She hid herself in a rose arbor and sobbed and croaked her heart out until the kitchen cat came by and asked her what the matter was.

"I'm in love with a handsome prince who wants to marry me. But first I must learn to sing, as I can no longer sing a note."

"Don't you worry about that," said the kitchen cat. "I have the best voice for miles around. Meet me at moonrise each evening and I'll soon teach you to sing again."

And so, by the light of the moon, the princess had singing lessons from the kitchen cat. At the end of the month he pronounced her perfectly in pitch, and said she was sure to please the prince this time.

Well, you can imagine what happened. The prince began to play his flute and the princess started to sing. But the sound that came from her mouth was an ear-piercing, spine-shattering H-O-W-L !

And the court laughed until their sides ached. The prince did not laugh but departed as before, vowing that he would give the princess only one more chance. And the King of Cats did not laugh either. He followed the sound from the other side of a forest and fell straightaway in love with her.

This time the princess ran away to a wood where she could cry her heart out in peace. But she woke up an owl, who asked her what the matter was.

The princess told her story. "We'll soon put that right," said the owl. "I've got a voice that charms the birds off the trees. Meet me at midnight every night and I'll soon teach you to sing once more."

So every midnight in the wood the princess took singing lessons from the owl.

"There," said the owl at last. "You too can charm the birds off the trees. You should certainly be able to charm a prince."

At the next banquet, when the princess opened her beautiful mouth to sing, the sound that came from her throat was the shrillest, sharpest TOO-WHIT-TOO-WHOO!

Although they tried to stop themselves, everyone fell off their chairs, howling and hooting with laughter. They laughed until the tears rolled, such cruel tears of mockery. How the princess blushed! How humiliated she felt!

But the Owl King in the forest heard her and fell straight off his treetop in love.

This time the princess ran so far into the dark forest that she was lost. Now this part of the forest was enchanted, and it was here that the princess, worn out with misery and hunger, fell asleep.

The Frog King eyed her from an enchanted pool. The King of Cats gazed at her from beside an enchanted stone. The Owl King blinked at her from an enchanted tree.

Then a strange sound began, a clear and beautiful sound. It was a human voice! It sang so finely and so sweetly, a melody as

light as air, that it woke up the princess. Although she did not know it, it was Chantelle's own voice. Stolen by the peevish aunt and let loose out of the window, the voice had sung its way to the enchanted forest. Now it worked its charm on the princess and she could truly hear again.

"Oh, I would give everything to have a voice like that," sighed the princess.

"Be mine and you shall!" croaked the Frog King, wishing she was a frog.

"Be mine and you shall!" howled the King of Cats, wishing she was a cat.

"Be mine and you shall!" hooted the Owl King, wishing she was an owl.

In that instant the lovely voice was hers again. But in this

enchanted forest, wishes had a dangerous way of coming true. As she sang, she changed. She lost her human form. Instead, she was the color of a frog, with the fur of a cat and the shape of an owl! Only her eyes were her own.

The Owl King screeched in dismay, the Frog King croaked in disgust, the King of Cats slunk away in distaste. And when Chantelle went to drink in the enchanted pool, she wept to see what she had become.

Now she could sing better than any human being alive, to the lyre, to the lute, and the flute. But what prince would want her now? What use would she be to anyone? With her own wings she soared through the forest, her singing more beautiful by day than the lark's, more beautiful by night than the nightingale's.

It so happened that the very same prince went hunting with his men in the forest one day. He was full of remorse at the disappearance of Princess Chantelle and had given up hope of finding her. So, when he heard this beautiful voice he made a vow.

"I gave up the princess I loved for a voice," he said. "Now, here is a beautiful voice. Whoever owns it, whether she is young or old, wise or foolish, fair or foul, I will marry her. Catch her by whatever means you can." And because it was an enchanted forest, where wishes came strangely true, the huntsmen caught Chantelle in the first trap they set and brought her before the prince, so changed that he did not know her.

She sat in a gilded cage, singing and singing, a creature so weird and wonderful that the prince could only stare at her in appalled fascination. But a prince must keep his word. Without

more ado, he married the
strange creature and took her back to the palace.

But she did not sit on the throne as his princess. Instead
she was locked in a tower at the very top of the palace, there to
sing her heart out, filling the palace and its grounds with her
beautiful melodies. The prince listened and was enchanted, for in
the sound was a vision of the beautiful Princess
Chantelle.

"If only I had married her," he kept saying to
himself. "How happy I should be. But I asked for
everything. So now I have my just rewards. I am married
to a voice, nothing but a voice. I have to make the best of it."

Because the prince could not bear to look at the strange
creature, he hired a keeper to take care of her. And it happened
that this keeper was none other than the peevish aunt who had
cast a spell on the princess. She recognized the eyes and the
voice of Chantelle and she had an evil thought.

"What a waste of a handsome prince! What a waste of a
beautiful voice! If only I could steal the voice for myself the

prince might marry me instead. But first I must get rid of this monster."

She fed poisoned food to the strange creature, day after day, little bit by little bit, until at last the creature fell into a deep sleep from which nothing could awaken it.

"We must take it back to the heart of the forest where we found it," said the prince. "There, it might revive."

They went in solemn procession, the princess carried on a bier to the middle of the enchanted forest, the peevish aunt keeping watch.

"One last dose of poison," she said to herself, "and all that is hers shall be mine."

But the Owl King in his treetop heard her. The Frog King on his lily pad heard her. The King of Cats in the undergrowth heard her.

"You want what the princess has," they said, "you shall have it!"

Because this was a place where wishes had a dangerous way of coming true, no sooner was this uttered than the strange creature turned back into the Princess Chantelle, as warm and alive and human as on the last day the prince had seen her. At the same time the peevish aunt's neck began to bulge like a frog's, her voice began to hiss like a cat's and her face became as sharp as an owl's. She screamed with rage and tore through the forest, never to be seen again.

The prince looked at his beloved princess and said, "What a fool I have been. Can you ever forgive me?"

Princess Chantelle did forgive him, and when she opened her

mouth to sing, the sound that came out of her beautiful throat was the voice that had been let loose into the enchanted forest. It was her own true voice, so happy to have found its owner that it la-laad and tra-laad, as merrily as could be.

SOMETHING ABOUT THE AUTHORS AND THEIR STORIES

The Paper Garden: **Tony Ramsay** is a playwright, journalist, and educationalist. For this, his first story for children, he was inspired by willow-pattern plates, Japanese art, and the literary tradition of portraying the East as "Elsewhere." "At the heart of the story is an ecological message—the cycle of death and regeneration."

★

Dancing in the Air: **Joan Aiken** is a *Guardian* newspaper award-winning writer for children. She came across the folk dance that features in this story when visiting Barcelona, Spain. "I walked out of my hotel in the old part of the town and found people dancing this wonderful dance, the Sardana, in the main square."

★

The Prince with Three Fates: **Ann Turnbull** has been writing for children for over a decade. Her story is a retelling of a tale translated from a papyrus fragment now housed in the British Museum.* "It is an ancient Egyptian folktale usually called *The Doomed Prince*. The original story is incomplete and I have supplied my own ending."

(* Reproduced in *Ancient Egyptian Literature*, Vol. 2 by Miriam Lichtheim, University of California, 1974)

★

The Queen of the Bees: **Vivian French** is a storyteller and writer of children's plays as well as stories. In this adaptation of *The Queen Bee*, one of the Grimms' fairy tales, she has turned the original tale on its head by recounting the exploits of three princess sisters: "In the Grimm retelling there are three princes, the youngest brother being a dwarf."

★

The Witch's Ride: **Jane Yolen** is a respected author known for her finely-crafted fairy tales. She drew inspiration for this story from an account of a seventeenth-century witchcraft trial: "As I read it, an opening for a story of my own began. I grafted that bit of real history onto an old folktale that I had read long ago about a man who was ridden like a horse by his witch wife."*

(* Reproduced in *Pale Hecate's Team* by Katherine M. Briggs)

★

The Snake Princess: **Jamila Gavin** started writing when she found few children's books reflecting different ethnic origins. Her story is a retelling of an old Punjabi folktale first published in *Tales of the Punjab* by Flora Annie Steel in 1894. "During the twenty-two years Steel lived in India, she collected a fabulous treasure of folktales, told to her in the great oral tradition of village India."

★

Chantelle, the Princess Who Could Not Sing: **Joyce Dunbar** taught English for twenty years before becoming a full-time writer. Her inspiration for stories usually begins with an image: "In this case, it was a sculpture by Picasso of an owl with the face of a beautiful woman.* Quite bewitching! I linked this to my own painful discovery as a child that the effect of my singing on other people was to make them hoot with mirth or cover their ears."

(* Chouette à tête de femme)